The angel said, "Mary, God is pleased with you. You will have a baby. You must name him Jesus. He will be the Son of God!

Joseph was a carpenter who loved Mary very much. One night while he was sleeping, an angel of the Lord visited him. This time the angel came in a dream.

The angel said, "Joseph, Mary and you are to be married. Mary will have a baby. Her baby will be God's Son. Name him Jesus."

When the baby Jesus was about to be born, Mary and Joseph had to take a long trip. The king wanted to count the people in his land. So Mary and Joseph traveled to Bethlehem to be counted. They were very tired when they got to Bethlehem.

Mary and Joseph tried to find a room at an inn, but it was too full.

There was only one place left for Joseph and Mary to sleep. They had to stay in a stable where animals lived!

That night God's one and only Son was born! Mary and Joseph named the baby Jesus. Mary lovingly wrapped the baby in strips of cloth to keep him warm.

That same night there were shepherds out in the fields taking care of their sheep. Suddenly an angel appeared to them!

At first the shepherds were
frightened, but the angel said,
"Do not be afraid. I bring you good
news of great joy. A Savior has been
born to you. He is Christ the Lord." Then the
sky was full of angels singing and praising God.

The shepherds found Baby Jesus lying in a manger. When the shepherds looked at Jesus, they praised God for him.

Some wise men followed a very bright star to Jesus. When the wise men saw Jesus, they were filled with joy.

The wise men bowed down and praised God for his Son, Jesus. Then they opened their treasures and gave gifts to Him.

God loves you so much that He gave you the greatest gift ever given—His one and only Son, Jesus.

"God loved the world so much that he gave his one and only Son. Anyone who believes in him will not die but will have eternal life."

John 3:16
NIrV/1998